Songs on the Vanilla Trail

LULLABIES AND NURSERY RHYMES FROM EAST AND SOUTHERN AFRICA

Songs collected by Nathalie Soussana
Musical arrangements by Jean-Christophe Hoarau
Illustrations by Magali Attiogbé

1 Une tite fleur l'amour
RÉUNION

A little flower of love
Beauty of a thousand birds
My sweet little rose-apple
How I love you!

2 Mbube

SOUTH AFRICA

Every morning you bring us luck
You are a lion, Mama

3 Matúwe
MOZAMBIQUE

Dance the matúwe
Dance my son
Dance my daughter
Dance right now

4 Jambo bwana

KENYA

Good day, sir
Kenya welcomes you
Dear visitor
Everything's fine

5 Ye tsodja waye

COMOROS

He comes alone
Don't let your brother die or sink
You will overcome, you will be saved
All who overcome are saved

6 Iny hono izy

MADAGASCAR

Here is the child, little bird
Take him with you into the fields
Take him high into the heavens
Bring him home when he is calm

7 Plouf
RÉUNION

A little lad
At the top of the tree
Takes off his undies
To poop

8 Dodo Siya
RÉUNION

Sleep Siya
This is not my house
I cannot sleep
I will look for a wife
For myself

9 Thula baba

SOUTH AFRICA

Hush little man
Papa will be back in the morning
A star will show him the way home

10 Owa mtrotro

COMOROS

Hush, my darling
The enemy's sun has set
Hush my darling
Your sun is now rising

11 Ntakana ntyilo
SOUTH AFRICA

Little chirping bird
What do you have in your beak?
I have never seen such a small bird
Carry water in its mouth

12 Kosa la manz ladan
RÉUNION

My little rooster, what did you eat?
A guava
A ripe fig
Blackberries
A voavanga
A potato

Dodo la minette
RÉUNION

Sleep little kitten
If she doesn't sleep
A big wild cat
Is going to catch her

Zan Batis
RÉUNION

Jean-Baptiste went fishing
His penknife in his pocket
To cut some fine shrimp

13 Mandihiza rahitsikitsika
MADAGASCAR

Show us your dance
We want to learn it
After the rains and the harvest

14 Café grillé
RÉUNION

Give me roasted coffee
The colour of my mother

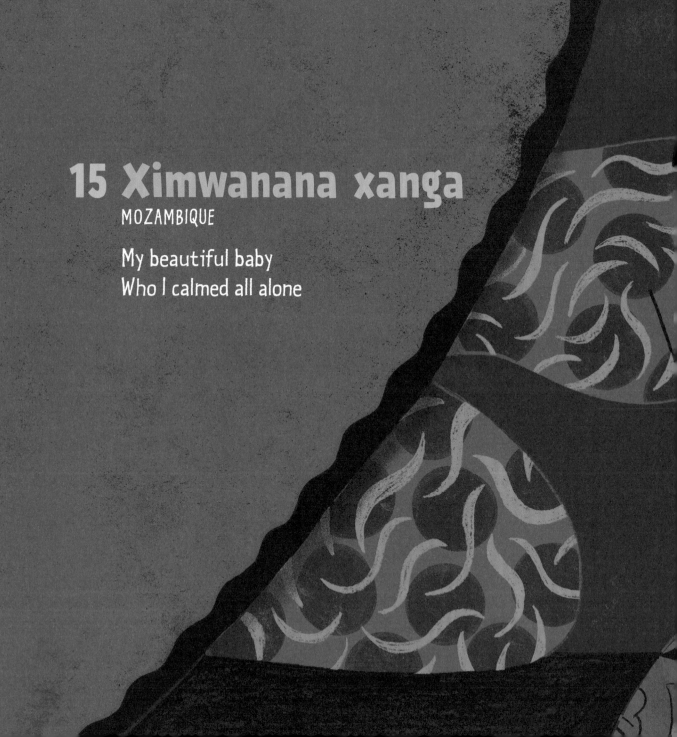

15 Ximwanana xanga

MOZAMBIQUE

My beautiful baby
Who I calmed all alone

16 Mandry ve

MADAGASCAR

Is the village sleeping?
Wake up, come and play!

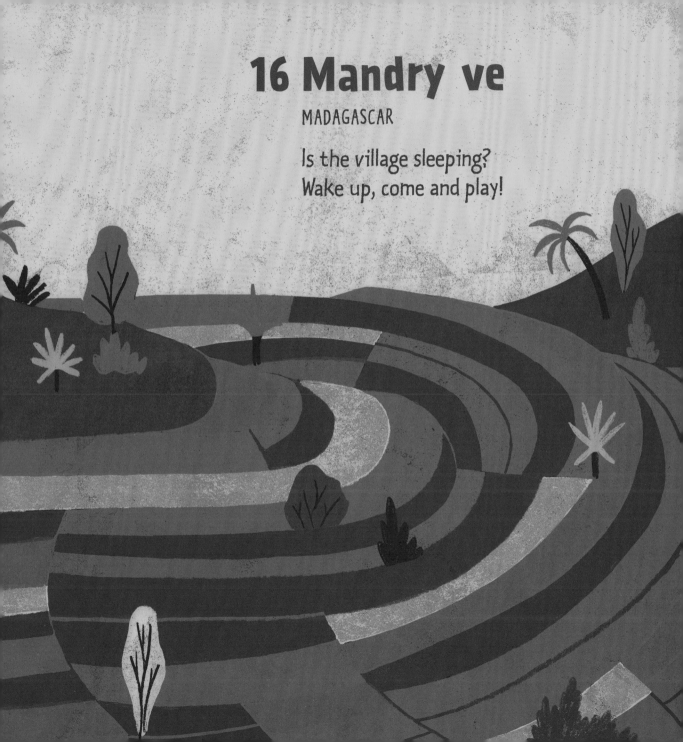

17 Frère Jacques
18 MADAGASCAR • RÉUNION • SOUTH AFRICA • MAYOTTE

Are you sleeping, Brother John?
Set the bells a-ringing
Time to rise
The rooster is singing

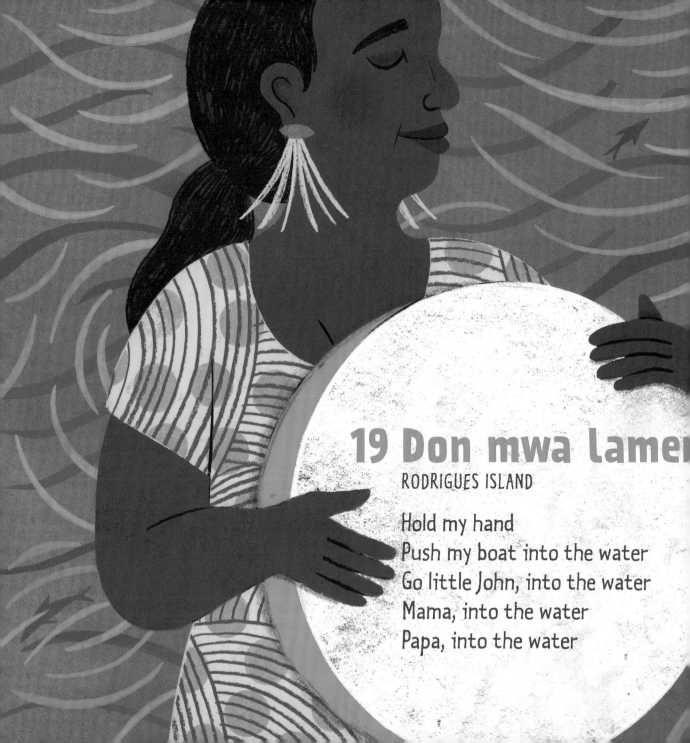

19 Don mwa lamer

RODRIGUES ISLAND

Hold my hand
Push my boat into the water
Go little John, into the water
Mama, into the water
Papa, into the water

20 Diavolana

MADAGASCAR

Round full moon at dusk
Never angry, always smiling
Light the way

21 Radjabu

COMOROS

Mama, give me some money
Mama, I have no money

22 **Ti marmit**

MAURITIUS

There's a small cauldron
With a small black hen dancing in it
1, 2, 3 goes my aunt
4, 5, 6 arithmetic
7, 8, 9 in my basket

23 Santa Amina

COMOROS

Saint Amina is the best
The best in the school
You don't even come close

24 Ny pangalana
MADAGASCAR

Paddle your canoe, my friend
To go fishing
Paddle

25 La rivière Tanier

MAURITIUS

I went by Lataniers River
Where I met an old grandma
I asked her what she was doing there
She said she was fishing chub
Alas, my children
One must work to earn one's living

From the shores of East Africa to the isles of the Indian Ocean

The slave trade had a powerful impact on islands in the Indian Ocean. Well before European colonists arrived, Indo-Malaysians, Indians, Chinese and Arabs were already sailing these waters, trading handcrafted objects and African slaves. With the arrival of the Portuguese, French and English in this part of the world, the practice of slavery multiplied. Four million people would be deported from Africa to Madagascar, the Comoros and the Mascarene Islands by the end of the nineteenth century. Today, the entire region bubbles over with the energy of these diverse influences. Each of these peoples brought their unique beliefs, rites, culture, language and collective memory. Now that these former colonies are independent, the Indian Ocean is home to a rich and disparate political, economic and cultural reality. Fully a part of the globalized world, the region looks to India or China and moves to the rhythm of Africa, but it is unlike any other place on the planet.

Why the title *Songs from the Vanilla Trail?*

Edmond Albius was an orphan born into slavery in 1829 on Bourbon Island (now Réunion). At the tender age of twelve, he made his name by discovering a practical technique for pollinating vanilla, an orchid whose pistil is worth its weight in gold! His technique would turn Réunion into the world's leading producer of vanilla for several decades. Then around 1880, plantation owners in Réunion introduced the process to Madagascar, which now produces 60% of the world's vanilla. When a group of islands in the Indian Ocean decided to join forces to tap into burgeoning international tourism, they launched a promotional campaign under the "Vanilla Islands" banner.

KENYA

KENYA
4 Jambo bwana

INDIAN OCEAN

TANZANIA

COMOROS
5   Ye tsodja waye
10 Owa mtrotro
21 Radjaɓu
23 Santa Amina

MAYOTTE
18 Frère Jacques

ZAMBIA

MOZAMBIQUE

ZIMBABWE

MADAGASCAR

MAURITIUS
22 Ti marmit
25 La riviere Tanier

BOTSWANA

RODRIGUES ISLAND
19 Don mwa lamen

MOZAMBIQUE
3   Matúwe tuwê
15 Ximwanana xanga

RÉUNION
1   Une tite fleur l'amour
7   Plouf
8   Dodo Siya
12 Kosa la manz ladan
12 Zan Batis
13 Dodo la minette
14 Café grillé
17 Frère Jacques

SOUTH AFRICA

SOUTH AFRICA
2   Mbube
9   Thula baba
11 Ntakana ntyilo
18 Frère Jacques

MADAGASCAR
6   Iny hono izy
13 Mandihiza rahitsikitsika
16 Mandry ve
17 Frère Jacques
20 Diavolana
24 Ny pangalana

The Comoro Islands

The four Comoro Islands—Ngazidja (*Grande Comore*), Mwalie (*Mohéli*), Ndzuwani (*Anjouan*) and Maore (*Mayotte*)—lie in the Mozambique Channel between Africa and Madagascar. Their name derives from the Arab *Juzur al-Qomor*, meaning "Islands of the Moon." Comorian is a Bantu language. The Comorian diaspor numbers 350,000, with some 200,000 islanders having settled in France.

The archipelago, which does not appear to have known human presence before the sixth century, has been populated over time by African Bantus, Austronesians, and Shirazi and Yemeni Arabs. In 1912, the islands became a French colony, attached to Madagascar up until 1946. In 1958, Comorians opted in a referendum to become an overseas territory of France and then went on to become independent in 1974. Mayotte alone rejected independence, and so separated politically from the other islands. Officially a French overseas *département* since 2011, Mayotte has diverse roots. The island's culture (traditionally matriarchal) and music incorporate African, Persian Arab, Indonesian, Malagasy and Western influences.

The Mascarene Islands

Located in the southwest Indian Ocean, the Mascarenes are an archipelago comprising three main islands (Réunion, Mauritius and Rodrigues) and several smaller islands. Réunion is a French département, while al the other islands form the Republic of Mauritius. Réunion was first inhabited by French colonists from Madagascar in 1665. A system of plantations, whose owners used slave labour, was organized to grow first coffee then sugar cane. After slavery was abolished in 1848, the colonial administration turned to India to hire indentured workers. Prior to becoming a French overseas *département* in 1946, Réunion was a land of former slaves and people of mixed descent. Inhabitants who had arrived from Africa, Europe and Asia had to build their own society and culture, and it was music and dance that brought them together The language of their songs was Réunion Creole, a blend of French, Malagasy, Tamil and Portuguese. They developed two forms of music and dance: *maloya* of African and Malagasy origin and *sega*, whose roots include European influences.

or a long time, Mauritius lay undiscovered and uninhabited. Arriving in the first half of the seventeenth century, the first colonists were Dutch. The island was later taken over by the French and then the British before becoming independent in 1968. English is the country's official administrative language, but French, taught from the age of four, is the language most spoken. Although Mauritian Creole is not officially recognized, it is spoken by a majority of the population and is the language of music and the arts. Creole descendants of African slaves, Hindu offspring of Indian workers, Tamils from southern India, Indian Muslims, a Chinese community and a small number of Europeans all cohabit Mauritius.

Of volcanic origin and the smallest of the archipelago's three main islands, Rodrigues is part of the Republic of Mauritius. Discovered in 1528 by Portuguese explorer Diogo Rodrigues, the island was only truly colonized in 1792, by settlers and their slaves from Isle de France (now Mauritius) and Bourbon Island (now Réunion). The current population of Rodrigues falls into two main groups: the majority Blacks of Malagasy and African origin and Mulattos (known as *Milat*) of mixed European and African heritage. Rodrigues has been independent since 2002. Unlike Mauritius and Réunion, it never developed a single-crop agriculture based on sugar cane, nor did it experience massive immigration of indentured Indian workers. The population therefore remains primarily Creole. Historic isolation and only recently emerging economic development have given Rodrigues an image of "authenticity" as an island where true Creole culture has been preserved.

Madagascar

Fifth largest island in the world, Madagascar (*Madagasikara* in Malagasy) is separated from Africa by the Mozambique Channel. Also known as the Great Red Island because of the lateritic soils colouring its plateaus, Madagascar is home to a range of civilizations and unique ecosystems. The people speak Malagasy, a Malayo-Polynesian language. The earliest settlers, either Malay or Indonesian, occupied the high plateaus in the island's interior, where they began growing rice in terraced plots. Later, Melanesian navigators settled the less hospitable coastal regions. In 1500, Portuguese explorer Diogo Dias became the first European to set foot on the island. When Africa was being sliced up among European colonizers, Madagascar was given to France in 1884. In 1960, the Republic of Madagascar became one of the region's first independent countries. It has a population of more than 25 million people of 18 distinct ethnicities. Current Madagascan literature is written in Malagasy or French, but the culture and music are often transmitted orally. Many traditional instruments, such as the valiha, are still played on festive holidays and at ceremonies. With roots in Afro-Asiatic rhythms and polyphonies, the main genres of Malagasy music and dance are afindrafindrao and salegy.

South Africa

South Africa boasts a great diversity of landscapes and peoples. Many languages, beliefs, traditions and social systems coexist here. The first inhabitants were the San. They were colonized in the twelfth century by the Khoikhois, who the Dutch called Hottentots (stutterers) because of the frequent clicking sounds in their language. They, in turn, were progressively pushed out by Bantus, starting in the seventeenth century. In 1652, the Dutch founded Cape Town as the nucleus of a new colony. They would be joined by French Protestant emigrants after the Edict of Nantes was revoked in 1685. In 1814, the Cape Town colony was annexed by the United Kingdom. Years of confrontation followed between the Boers (descendants of Franco-Dutch settlers) and the British. After the Union of South Africa was established in 1910, the situation worsened for Blacks, Indians and people of mixed race, culminating in the 1948 implementation of a segregationist policy known as Apartheid. This shameful, bloody policy would remain the law of the land until it was abolished in 1991. The diversity of South Africans and their history is reflected in their languages, eleven of which have been officially recognized since the end of Apartheid. Afrikaans, a mixed language based in Dutch, is spoken by 14% of the population, while English, the language of the government, is spoken by 9%. The rest of the population uses traditional Bantu languages, of which the most common are Zulu (23%) and Xhosa (18%).

Mozambique

Mozambique owes its name to Sultan Sofana Musa Mbeki, contemporary of Portuguese explorer Vasco a Gama. The population, primarily of Bantu origin, comprises about ten groups unevenly distributed cross the large country. Mozambique was not actually colonized by Portugal until the end of the ineteenth century. The country became independent in 1975 under a socialist government. The eighbouring countries of Rhodesia (now Zimbabwe) and South Africa, still ruled by Whites, began war of destabilization that would ruin Mozambique. In 1992, after more than 15 years of war, the ountry found peace and economic recovery by renouncing socialism and successfully negotiating with he RENAMO guerillas, although it remains one of the world's poorest nations. Like many other African ountries, Mozambique is multilingual. The official language, inherited from colonial times, is Portuguese Mozambique is the world's second largest Portuguese-speaking nation). Most indigenous languages are f Bantu origin. Some 43 of these are currently in use, including Ronga, spoken in Maputo and southern ozambique.

Kenya

enya is an East African country bisected by the equator. It is named after Mount Kenya, which the amba people call Kiinyaa (Mountain of the Ostrich), in reference to the black rocks and snowy white eaks reminiscent of the feathers of a male ostrich. The valley below is often called the "Cradle of umanity" because of the many hominid fossils that have been discovered there. Seventy tribal groups f different ethnicities live in Kenya. They speak about fifty different languages, some of which are isappearing. Spoken by 12 million people, Swahili is the lingua franca and co-official language of the ountry, together with English. It is a Bantu language influenced by Arab and found in about twenty ountries, primarily in East Africa and as far as the Comoro Islands.

Rich, highly mixed musical styles

Accompanying every aspect of life, music plays a vital role in a people's cultural identity. In East and Southern Africa, perhaps more than elsewhere, it is the glue holding societies together and generating fertile exchanges. Music draws inspiration from a great diversity of indigenous heritages blended with influences of the major colonizing countries. It serves as an audible "identity card" specifically pointing to a country, ethnicity, clan and even to a particular tribe. The Indian Ocean islands scattered off the coast of East Africa have been touched by many civilizations. Africa, naturally, but Asia, Oceania, the Islamic world and Europe have also impacted the history and identity of the Comoros, Madagascar, Mascarenes and other islands in the region. The resulting rich, highly mixed musical styles that are unique to each island may be melodious or rhythmic, nostalgic or joyful. They reflect historical and emotional diversity, and illustrate the capacity of a society to welcome new horizons through contact with others.

1 Une tite fleur l'amour RÉUNION

Language Réunion Creole **Singer** Éloïse Agenor-Poinsot

Vanilla is emblematic of Réunion, which by the end of the nineteenth century had become the world's leading producer of the only orchid with an edible fruit. With *Une tite fleur l'amour*, we make our first stop to visit what was once called Bourbon Island, a miniature Planet Earth, where Europe, Asia, the Arab world and Africa coexist. This is a delightful lullaby in Réunion Creole. Derived from French and influenced by idioms as diverse as Malagasy, Portuguese, Tamil and Norman, Réunion Creole (*réyoné*) is a veritable witness to the island's diversity. It is a language (*langaz*) abounding in images, born of the need for mutual comprehension between African and Malagasy slaves and their European plantation-owning masters. The tree referred to in th song—the *jambakka (jamalac)*, also known as wax apple and rose apple—is a tropical tree that produces attractive bell-shaped red fruit.

Dodo ti baba	Sleep, little baby
Sa zistoir maman avec son papa	This is the story of your Mama and your Papa
Une tite fleur l'amour, la belle au mil zoiseaux	A little flower of love, beauty of a thousand birds
Ti fill' jamalac com mi y'aime a ou	My sweet little rose-apple, how I love you!

2 **Mbube** SOUTH AFRICA

Language Zulu **Singer** Nolitha Dlabhongo

It is 1939 in Johannesburg, South Africa. Six young men are about to improvise what will become one of the most popular songs of the twentieth century. Soloman Linda, from the Natal region, sings a few notes before the other members of The Evening Birds join in. The improvisation is recorded and becomes known as *Mbube* (The Lion) in Zulu. The lion is a powerful, quasi-mystical figure (the Zulu people refer to Jesus as the "Lion of Judah"). The lyrics of the song, which undoubtedly recall lion hunts from Linda's Zulu childhood, were reworked a number of times as the song became an international success. The English version was popularized by Pete Seeger in 1952 as "*Wimoweh*" and was a No. 1 hit for The Tokens in 1961 as "*The Lion Sleeps Tonight*."

Mbube, also known as *isicathamiya* (ambush) in Zulu, references a vocal style born in the mines of South Africa in the early twentieth century in which Zulu chants are sung a cappella. The technique of *mbube* involves a kind of dialogue between the lead singer and back-up singers. The result is a popular musical style inhabited by the Zulu values of competition, strength, power and communication with ancestors. In South Africa, the song's rhythmic incantations have made it a lullaby to reassure children of their mother's presence, comparing her to a lion.

Njalo ekuseni uya waletha amathamsanqa	Every morning you bring us luck
Amathamsanqa	Good luck
Mbube ah, uyimbube ah, uyimbube ah, uyimbube ah	Lion, you are a lion, you are a lion, you are a lion
Hihihi hihihi hihihi… Uyimbube Mama yoh	Hihihi, hihihi, hihihi, you are a lion, Mama
Yoh Yoh Yoh… Uyimbube Mama yoh	Yoh, yoh, yoh, you are a lion, Mama
Hihihi hihihi hihihi… Uyimbube Mama yoh	Hihihi, hihihi, hihihi, you are a lion, Mama
Yoh Yoh Yoh… Uyimbube Mama yoh	Yoh, yoh, yoh, you are a lion, Mama

3 Matúwe tuwê MOZAMBIQUE

Language Ronga **Singer** Costa Neto

Matúwe tuwê is a dance song with a binary rhythm known as *xissaizana* found in southern Mozambique, especially in the capit
city of Maputo. *Matúwe* has no literal translation. It is found exclusively in the song of the same name and the accompanying
dance. Children form a circle as they sing the song and clap. In turn, they go to the middle of the circle and dance, turning to
the rhythm of *tuwê, tuwê*. The song is also used for a rope-skipping game. Two children swing the rope while the others form
a line and wait their turn to jump. As the song proceeds, more than one child jumps at the same time. Everyone waiting their
turn sings and claps.

A matúwe, tuwê tuwê	Dance the matúwe, tuwê tuwê
A matúwe, tuwela mwananga tuwê	Dance the matúwe; dance my son/my daughter, tuwê
Hi nga tuwela ka	So dance right now
Tuwê tuwê tuwê tuwê tuwê tuwê tuwê tuwê	Tuwê tuwê tuwê tuwê tuwê tuwê tuwê tuwê
Tuwela mwananga tuwê	Dance my son/my daughter, tuwê

4 Jambo bwana KENYA

Language Swahili **Singer** Kamay Pelasimba

This song was composed by Kenyan musician Teddy Kalanda Harrison as an enjoyable way to teach tourists to Mombasa a few
words of Swahili. *Jambo bwana* is now sung on every street corner to every tourist who happens by. It has almost become a
national anthem! The lyrics include a series of common greetings in Swahili: *Habari gani? Nzuri sana* ("How are you doing?"
"Very well!") and *Hakuna matata* ("Everything's fine!"). A melody that's easy to remember and repetitive words have made
the song very popular in Kenya and Tanzania. It is also enjoyed by children, who recognize *hakuna matata* from the Disney film
The Lion King. Swahili, mother tongue along the East African coastline, is one of the most important linguae francae on the
continent, where it has developed into distinctive regional variants.

Jambo, jambo bwana!	Good day, good day, sir!
Habari gani?	How are you?
Nzuri sana	Very well!
Wageni wakaribishwa	Visitors, you are welcome
Kenya yetu	To our Kenya
Hakuna matata	Everything's fine.

Ye tsodja waye COMOROS

Language Comorian Singer Nawal Mlanao

For centuries, the collective memory of Comorians has been handed down from generation to generation through song and dance. Music accompanies every stage of life. When a child is born, women sing poetic songs called *himbiya ikosa* to support the mother during labour. Comorian children are thus welcomed into the world by a kind of lullaby, the genre to which *Ye tsodja waye* belongs. The music of the Comoro Islands has been highly influenced by the world of Islam, exemplified by the chorus of women repeating *youyou* at the beginning of the song.

Ye tsodja waye
Ye karumu mndru
Lillahi udja waye
Ye karumu mndru

He comes alone
He's by himself
By God, he comes alone
He's by himself

Djawe yatsife na djawe yatsirore
Ngoshio ngama uondohe
Owashia ngama waondoha

Don't let your brother die or sink
You will overcome, you will be saved
All who overcome are saved

Iny hono izy MADAGASCAR

Language Malagasy Singer Tiana Masselot

As the Christian era was dawning, Austronesian explorers reached Madagascar on outrigger canoes. Arriving from islands and the austral coastline of Southeast Asia, they brought a culture related to that of the Philippines and Malaysia. For this reason, the Madagascar tube zither known as the *valiha* (from the Sanskrit *vacfya*) heard in this lullaby bears a remarkable resemblance to zithers played in Cambodia, Vietnam and the Philippines. Made of bamboo, the valiha is a symbol of Madagascar. Originally, the strings were long filaments of bamboo bark stretched over movable metallic frets. Several types of valiha are found in different regions, some diatonic, others chromatic. Justin Vali, heard performing here, is a specialist of the instrument, whose sound is reminiscent of the kora and harpsichord. Having learned from his father starting at the age of five, Vali went on to become an ambassador for Malagasy music, sharing stages all over the world with the likes of Peter Gabriel and Kate Bush.

Iny hono izy ravorombazaha
Ento manaraka anao any an-tsaha
Raha mitomany hampangino
Rehefa mangina avereno

Here is the child, little bird
Take him with you into the fields
If he cries, comfort him
Bring him home when he is calm

Iny hono izy ravorombazaha
Ento manaraka anao any an-tsaha
Ento misidina ambony
Rehefa mangina avereno

Here is the child, little bird
Take him with you into the fields
Take him high into the heavens
Bring him home when he is calm

7 Plouf RÉUNION

Language Réunion Creole **Singers** Lionel Agenor **and** Micheline Tamachia

A counting-out nursery rhyme is a spoken or sung rhythmic form traditionally used to count players in determining who remains in a game and who is eliminated. "Eenie meenie miney mo" in English, for instance. A player is touched with every syllable, and the fate of the last one touched is determined by the rules of the game. Creole nursery rhymes are perfect for prosodic games as they offer variation in rhythm and intonation, changes of tempo and expressive possibilities through volume, cadence and articulation. So here is a short collection of elimination nursery rhymes starting with a traditional plouf [splash]. Children have every opportunity to express their creativity in these language games, where humour, assonance and rhyming are more important than meaning.

Plouf	Splash
Un etiket Marie bonbec	A label, Marie Bonbon
Cari canet truc	Curry, marbles, stuff
C'est ma roulette qui roule très doux	My little wheel turns gently
Mon p'tit chewing-gum l'est doux	My chewing-gum is soft
Un ti bonom en l'air pié de boi	A little lad at the top of the tree
Tir son culott pou li caca	Takes off his undies to poop
La gom son 2 ti doi	He stuck two fingers in it

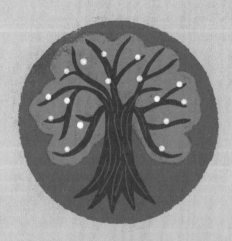

8 Dodo Siya RÉUNION

Language Réunion Creole **Singer** Lionel Agenor

This song is in the maloya style as typified by Firmin Viry's well-known *Valet, Valet*. When Viry was a young man, he heard maloya music every day played in the *kalbanon* (camps) where his parents and other rural workers stayed. Back from the fields at day's end, having eaten and quenched their thirst, the workers would take out their instruments for a "dust soirée" during which everyone would dance, have fun, and let out their feelings. A potpourri of traditional Creole songs to typical rhythms would follow one after the other. In this context, maloya served to represent social relations on the island, preserve a tradition in peril and attempt to define the Creole identity. This song features an emblematic figure of traditional Réunion maloya. She is an Indian woman known to all as Monmon Siya ("she who does not sleep in anyone else's house"), Siya (or Sita) is a central figure in the Hindu epic *Ramayana*, ascribed to the Indian poet Maharishi Valmiki. A *gaulette* was a measure of agricultural land in common use by inhabitants of Réunion up until the end of the twentieth century.

The song is accompanied by a kayamb (*kayanm*), an instrument from Mozambique introduced by plantation slaves. It is also played in Madagascar and Mauritius, where it is called *maravanne*. It is a rattle instrument in the idiophone family. A large rectangular frame of light wood is partitioned by two sugar cane stalks of equal length woven together. The stems are filled with seeds, small pieces of glass or coins, at the whim of the builder, that strike the walls when the instrument is shaken. The kayamb is completed with three fibre braids of *vacoa* (screw pine), a palm-like tree. The player shakes and rotates the kayamb energetically to produce its distinctive sound determined by the size of the sound box, as well as the quantity and quality of grains.

Dodo dodo Siya, la caze la pa mwin mi dodo pa	Sleep Siya, this is not my house, I cannot sleep
In coq in poule mwin nana	I have a rooster and a hen
100 gaulettes la terre ma na poin	A hundred gaulettes of land have I not
Malé rodé, malé rodé, malé rodé	I will look for, look for, look for
In fom pou moin	A wife for myself

9 Thula baba SOUTH AFRICA

Language Zulu Singer Nolitha Dlabhongo

This lullaby points to new realities in the Zulu lifestyle. Traditionally, men were farmers raising crops to feed the village, but nowadays there is little work in the places they can afford to live. It is almost impossible for fathers to both live with their children and support the family. A mother who has stayed in the village uses this lullaby to maintain hope that "the morning star will lead Papa home." The Zulus, whose name comes from *amazulu*, meaning "People of the Sky," are Bantu-speaking populations originally from East Africa. Their presence in South Africa dates back to the seventeenth century. They have assimilated many sounds from the San and Khoisan languages of the region's first inhabitants. As a result, Zulu and Xhosa have preserved click consonants from the now extinct source languages. Today, Zulus are South Africa's largest ethnic group, making up about 20% of the population.

Thula Thul, Thula baba, Thula sana	Hush, hush little man, hush my baby
Thula ubaba uzobuya ekuseni	Hush, Papa will be back in the morning
Kukhon Inkanyezi ziholel' ubaba	A star will show him the way home
Zimkhanyisel' indlela eziyekhaya	It will light his path
Sobe sikhona ngabonke bashoyo	All the way home
Bayathi buyela. Ubuye le khaya	Everyone will encourage him:
	"Come home," they will say
	He is back

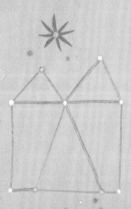

10 Owa mtrotro COMOROS

Language Comorian Singer Nawal Mlanao

In the Comoro Islands, lullabies are usually sung by the mother, a young aunt or an older sister. In addition to quieting and reassuring the child, a lullaby allows the adult to reflect on the past, present and future, mirroring society and the mother–child relationship. In this lullaby, we hear the mother express her own anguish and pain as sleep eludes her. Yet the promise of divine protection and blessing ensures the child feels secure. She also reminds the child that it is her duty to live up to the parents' expectations and not disappoint them: "And tomorrow it will be your turn to take care of us."

Owa is a term of endearment, of tenderness. This lullaby, which includes some words of Swahili, is also sung in Congo by Bantu populations.

Owa mtrotro	Hush, my child
Mwana wa ɓaraka	Blessed child
Mwana shilizi kalala	A child who won't stop crying can't sleep
Ɓiɓi ye! Owa!	My darling! Hush!
Na mamahe kamuladza, ɓiɓi ye	For your Mama can't sleep either, darling
Nirenge upvi mwalangu	Which to choose, O Lord?
Ɓiɓi ye! Owa!	My darling! Hush!
Nilishe upvi mwalangu, ɓiɓi ye	Which to leave behind, O Lord, my darling
Musindre tsi Mungu wangu	My enemy is not my God
Ɓiɓi ye! Owa!	My darling! Hush!
Kanipva kanipvoshea, ɓiɓi ye	He neither gives me away nor takes me back, my darling
Ahitutu ahitutu	My little darling, my little darling
Ɓiɓi ye! Owa!	My darling! Hush!
Rua mwana usilie, ɓiɓi ye	Stop crying, my child
Risimia rihuleye mwanangu, owa	We ask God to raise you, my child, hush
Ata meso urileye, ɓiɓi ye	And tomorrow it will be your turn to take care of us, my darling
Jua la musindre litso	The enemy's sun has set
Ɓiɓi ye! Owa!	My darling! Hush!
Laho lisihea pvasa, ɓiɓi ye	Your sun is now rising, my darling

11 Ntakana ntyilo SOUTH AFRICA

Language Xhosa Singer Melissa Peter

This is a very old traditional song, in which the woman, considered to be a protectress, is compared to a small chirping bird. She takes care of the family by providing milk, for her babies, and water, which is critical to survival. Xhosa is a tonal language like Chinese. South Africa alone has more than 8 million speakers (about 18% of the population), making it the second most spoken language after Zulu. The "xh" in Xhosa, a consonant unique to the language, is an aspirated lateral alveolar click. This means that the sound is produced by a slight click of the tongue to one side (similar to a sound used by equestrians in Europe to calm their horse), followed by an audible breath.

Ntakana ntyilo ntyilo ntyilo
Uphethe ntoni ngomlonyana?

Little chirping bird
What do you have in your beak, singing bird?

Ndaze ndayibon' intak' encinane
Ipheth' amasi ngomlonyana

For I have never seen such a small bird
Carry water, carry milk in its mouth

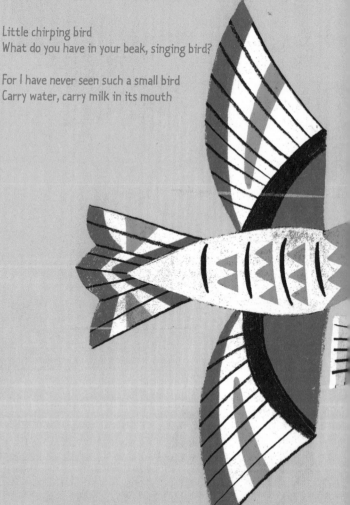

12 Kosa la manz ladan · Zan Batis
Dodo la minette   RÉUNION

Language Réunion Creole **Singers** Lionel Agenor **and** Micheline Tamachia

This sequence of two nursery rhymes and a lullaby begins with the finger game *Kosa la manz ladan*. The child's hand is opened (*inn i rouv la min*) and a finger placed in the middle of her palm (*inn i mèt son dwa dann milyé*). Now the rhyme is recited and the child's palm tickled to the words *Kosa la manz laden?* Each fruit named corresponds to a finger: guava for the thumb, ripe fig for the index finger, and so on up to the little finger. *Patat. La pi? A pi!* (A patato. Is that all? That's all!)

Together with Ti Zan and Ti Kok, Zan Batis is an emblematic figure in Réunion. He is a daring and resourceful young boy whose exploits are recounted in this action song. He goes down to the river to fill his basket with shrimp, carrying with him a penknife (*in ti kouto*), a gift traditionally offered to a boy to mark the transition to manhood. *Yango* means "beautiful" in Réunion Creole. The sense here is of beautiful large red shrimp.

Dodo la minette is one of the best-known lullabies in Réunion. The main idea is always the same but the details vary from one region and cultural identity to another. Versions include "*Dodo Ninette, Sainte Elizabeth*" and "*Dodo la minette, Catherinette.*"

The word *marron* could be translated as "wild." The term comes from maroon slaves who escaped to freedom. Tired and weary of staying on their feet to rock a child to sleep, the mother, grandmother or wet-nurse would end up invoking the arrival of a wildcat—not necessarily the best way to help a child fall asleep! *Zan Batis* and *Dodo la minette* are examples of the sega music genre, the best known and most common in Réunion.

Kosa la manz ladan

Ti kok, kosa la manz ladan? Gouyav   My little rooster, what did you eat? A guava
Ti kok, kosa la manz ladan? Fig mir   My little rooster, what did you eat? A ripe fig
Ti kok, kosa la manz ladan? Méryé   My little rooster, what did you eat? Blackberries
Ti kok, kosa la manz ladan? Vavang   My little rooster, what did you eat? A voavanga
Ti kok, kosa la manz ladan? Patat   My little rooster, what did you eat? A potato
La pi? A pi!   Is that all? That's all!

Zan Batis

Zan Batis la parti la pès   Jean-Baptiste went fishing
Son ti kouto dann son posèt   His penknife in his pocket
Pou koupé yango sovrèt   To cut some fine shrimp
Pou koupé yango sovrèt   To cut some fine shrimp

Dodo la minette

Dodo la minette   Sleep little kitten
L'enfant de Jeannette   Daughter of Jeannette
Si la minette y dodo pas   If the kitten doesn't sleep
Chat' marron va souke a li   A big wild cat is going to catch her

13 Mandihiza rahitsikitsika MADAGASCAR

Language Malagasy Singers Tao Ravao and Tiana Masselot

This traditional song, also known as "Dance of the Kestrel" (a diurnal bird of prey), owes its name to the Malagasy kestrel's unique hunting technique. As though it were suspended by a line, the bird beats its wings vigorously without moving as it surveys the land below to the right and to the left. This technique resembles a Malagasy dance style that involves shaking the shoulders, arms and hands without moving the feet. The song uses onomatopoeias mimicking the kestrel's cry.

The word *fararano* is the month of March, which brings the end of the rainy season and the start of the rice harvest. It is also the traditional Malagasy month of the New Year. Mahamasina is a major sacred site in Antananarivo, where kings and queens would address the people. The *Rova de Manjakamiadana* (Palace of the Queen) was the official residence of Madagascar sovereigns in the nineteenth century.

Mandihiza rahitsikitsika	Show us your dance, Lady Kestrel
Hianaranay hianaranay	After the rains and the harvest
Mandihiza rahitsikitsika	Show us your dance, Lady Kestrel
Hianaranay amin' ny fararano	So we can learn it after the rains and the harvest
Mandihiza mandihiza mandihiza rahitsikitsika	Dance, dance, dance, Lady Kestrel
Mandihiza ry Mahamasina	Dance, citizens of Mahamasina
Mifalia Manjakamiadana	Be joyful, citizens of Manjakamiadana
Mandihiza rahitsikitsika	Show us your dance, Lady Kestrel
Hianaranay amin' ny fararano	So we can imitate you after the rains and the harvest
Mandihiza mandihiza mandihiza rahitsikitsika	Dance, dance, dance, Lady Kestrel

14 Café grillé RÉUNION

Language Réunion Creole **Singer** Lionel Agenor

The word *maloya* in the lyrics refers to a musical genre, a style of singing and a type of dance. Originally, maloya was used to call upon the spirits in rituals honouring the ancestors. It incorporates musical practices brought to the island by slaves, indentured workers and French colonists. Sung by slaves out of their master's hearing when the day's work was done as a means of helping them endure and resist, maloya employs a single voice echoed by a chorus to express pain, suffering and nostalgia.

The music is supported by traditional percussion instruments, the rouleur (*roulèr*), kayamb, piker and, in this case, the bobre (*bob*). The bobre, cousin of the Brazilian berimbau, is a musical bow of varying size. Of African origin, it has a calabash resonator at the base fixed on one side to a bow and open on the other to emit vibrations downwards. The musician holds the bow against their body and strikes the string in rhythm with a stick (*batavék*), which has a small pouch (*kavir*) on the end made of screw pine fibre. The pouch contains seeds that resonate when the stick strikes the string. The result is two simultaneous sound sources: rhythm from the rattling of the seeds in the kavir (similar to maracas) and the primary sound of the vibrating string that the musician amplifies or muffles by controlling the opening in the calabash.

Donn a mwin mon café grillé	Give me roasted coffee
Café grillé koulèr mo momon	Coffee roasted the colour of my mother
La la la la la la la	La la la la la la la
Maloya lapa nou lafé	We did not invent the maloya
Gramounn lontan la fé maloya	Our ancestors invented the maloya
La la la la la la la	La la la la la la la.

15 Ximwanana xanga MOZAMBIQUE

Language Ronga **Singer** Costa Neto

The mother speaks to the absent father in this lullaby: "You appreciate, don't you, that I calmed our child by myself?" Once the baby has been calmed, the lullaby ends with the traditional "wo, wo, wo" until the child has fallen asleep. Nowadays, this song is performed by various musical groups in the marrabenta style, a very popular urban musical genre that developed in southern Mozambique, specifically in the Mafalala neighbourhood of Maputo, in the 1930s. Performers such as Fany Mpfumo and Dilon Djindji use it to create protest dance songs. Marrabenta is inspired by traditional Mozambican music and more modern rhythms from South Africa and is a musical genre on a par with maloya and sega. Invented in Mozambique during the colonial period, marrabenta was at first intended to entertain colonists and was played on international instruments by musicians with no formal training. Later on, they would use anything at hand, including steel oil drums, pieces of wood and fishing line. The word *marrabenta* comes from the verb *rebentar* (*arrebentar* in the vernacular), a Portuguese word meaning "to break" or "burst." The musicians "break" the rhythm on their guitar. During the struggle for liberation, the Portuguese banned marrabenta for being subversive.

Ximwanana xanga xa ku xonga	My beautiful baby
Ni n'gô psala vupsanga	Who I calmed all alone
A hi n'txumu	It doesn't matter
Wa dlembula n'kata	You appreciate it, my husband
Wa dlembula	You appreciate it

16 Mandry ve MADAGASCAR

Language Malagasy **Singer** Tiana Masselot

Mandry ve ny ao an-tanàna is a popular Merina song from the late nineteenth century. Performed at festivities marking the rice harvest, it served to call villagers to work. Descendants of Madagascar's Asian peoples, the Merina ("those who inhabit the highlands") live on the island's central plateaus near the capital city of Antananarivo..

Mandry ve ny ao an-tanàna e ?	Is the village sleeping?
Izy efa matory ô	It's already asleep.
Mifohaza hilalao e	Wake up, come and play!

Frère Jacques

MADAGASCAR • RÉUNION • SOUTH AFRICA • MAYOTTE

Languages Malagasy, Réunion Créole, Xosa **and** Maore Comorian **Singers** Tiana Masselot, Éloïse Agenor-Poinsot, Nawal Mlanao **and** Melissa Peter

Here is a potpourri of different versions of the world's best-known French nursery rhyme. Dating from the eighteenth century (attributed nowadays to Jean-Philippe Rameau), *Frère Jacques* has found its way into more than a hundred languages. The original words refer to the office of Matins, sung at night's end just before Lauds, marking the break of day. During Matins, a monk rings the bells. Here he is called Yangu, Zak or Zaka. Echoing the original text ("Brother John, Brother John, Wake up! Wake up!"), the Réunion version adds the story of a rooster who sings "pretty Mama"! Over the course of history, this nursery rhyme has inspired other words around the world, with Jacques becoming John, Ahmed or Bouki. In languages such as Mandarin and Vietnamese, the text has changed from sacred to profane to evoke (respectively) a tiger that has lost its tail and the flight of a butterfly. In Thai, the rhyme has been transposed into a finger game and has almost nothing in common with the original!

In Malagasy

Rahalahy Zaka	Are you sleeping?
Matory ve ianao?	Brother John
Ampanenoy ny lakolosy	Set the bells a-ringing
Ding ding dong	Ding, dang, dong

In Réunion Creole

Konpèr Zak	Brother John
Lèv aou	Time to rise
Kok la pou santé, bèl manman	The rooster is singing, pretty Mama
Kok la pou santé	The rooster is singing
Ding dang dong	Ding, dang, dong

In Xhosa

Mntakwethu	Are you sleeping?
Ulele na?	My brother
Vuk' ubethi ntsimbi	Wake up to the bell
Kelegenkqe	Ding, dang, dong

In Maore Comorian

Mwananyangu	Are you sleeping?
Ulala?	My brother
Namsone les matines	Ring the bells for Matins
Ding dang dong	Ding, dang, dong

19 Don mwa lamen RODRIGUES ISLAND

Language Rodriguan Creole **Singers** Jean Groeme and Hélène Groeme

Don mwa lamen is a sega tambour, a festive song that was traditionally performed during evening village gatherings on Rodrigues. The song comprises a single short melody sung by the "composer" and repeated by the chorus. The simplicity of the text and melody make it possible for children nowadays to include the song in their repertoire of dance games. Originally associated with rebellion and resistance, sega tambour facilitated conflict resolution, encouraged socialization and strengthened relationships, with the lyrics and dance playing a central role. The accompaniment was played on ravanne drums, which are the soul of sega. Normally made from the skin of goats, this large drum lends sega its distinct rhythmic identity. Slaves originally from the Mozambican coast and now living on Indian Ocean islands called this genre *tchéga*. Original sega often had a spiritual function. The dancers would enter into a trance to the muffled rhythm of the ravanne—a magical altered state known as *babani* used to invoke spirits of the dead. Sega tambour is one of two forms of sega practised in Rodrigues, the other being segakordeon, played on diatonic accordions that are somewhat reminiscent of bagpipes.

Don mwa lamen, pus mo bato, dan delo	Hold my hand, push my boat into the water
Ayo mo piti Zan, dan delo ô	Go little John, into the water, ho!
Dan delo mama, dan delo papa, dan delo	Into the water, Mama, into the water, Papa, into the water
Ayo mo piti Zan, dan delo	Go little John, into the water, ho!
Ayo mo karazan, dan delo ô	Go my dear John, into the water, ho!
Dan delo mama, dan delo papa, dan delo	Into the water, Mama, into the water, Papa, into the water

20 Diavolana MADAGASCAR

Language Malagasy **Singer** Tao Ravao

The full moon is always highly anticipated by the Malagasy as a bearer of peace and harmony. On these special nights that occu but every 29 days according to the lunar calendar used by the Elders of Madagascar, children were allowed to play outside until late. Generally, they gathered in the yard to dance a farandole to the tune of *Diavolana fenomanana* (Happy beneath the full moon) and then play various games together until sleep overcame them. It was believed that evil spirits are powerless to harm the living during a full moon, so the children were in no danger!

Diavolana fenomanana takariva re	Round full moon at dusk
Tsy mba sosotra fa mirana lava	Never angry, always smiling
Ombay lalana	Light the way
Ombay lalana Befelatanana	Light the way to Befelatanana

21 Radjaɓu COMOROS

Language Comorian **Singer** Ahlam Boina

This round danced in school yards emphasizes the importance of family relations as a system of social identity. The principle of kinship in the Comoros is related, on one hand, to ancient customs and, on the other, to the influence of Islam. Children bear the father's name in keeping with Koranic rules but live in the mother's house in accordance with the ancestral principle of matrilineal filiation. This round dance also refers to the abject poverty of many families.

Ra ra Radjaɓu
Radjaɓu wa Ali
Na Kamari wa Dini
Na Ali wa Hasani
Emazofera
La la la la la...
Mama kunipve pesa!
Mama ntsina pesa

Ra ra Radjaɓu
Radjaɓu, son of Ali
And Kamari, son of Dini
And Ali, son of Hasani
Are drivers
La la la la la...
Mama, give me some money!
Mama, I have no money

22 Ti marmit MAURITIUS

Language Mauritian Creole **Singer** Ahlam Boina

This nursery rhyme is very popular on Mauritius. It was first recorded in 2002 by the *Association pour le bien-être des aveugles de l'île Maurice* (ABAIM, an association for the blind) with the children (*ti marmit*) of Saturday Care. Since then, *Ti marmit*, which is based on a sega rhythm, can be heard in school yards, at festivities and during marriages. Like maloya in Réunion, sega is rooted in the suffering of slaves, and also has links to revolt and communities of runaway slaves. It played a key role in the early process of creolization.

Ti éna ene ti marmit
Enn ti poule noir ti danse ladan
Li apiye ar ros cari
Alala Moana ki ti fer sa
Moana, Moana, Moana conne pik séga
1 2 3 roulé matante
4 5 6 mathématique
7 8 9 dan mo panier

There's a small cauldron
With a small black hen dancing in it
She's leaning on the curry stone
Alala, Moana's doing it
Moana, Moana, Moana knows how to dance the sega
1, 2, 3 goes my aunt
4, 5, 6 arithmetic
7, 8, 9 in my basket

23 Santa Amina COMOROS

Language Comorian **Singer** Nawal Mlanao

Santa Amina is a round dance performed by girls in Comorian school yards. Standing in a circle, they sing and clap their hands. The leader calls a child by their first name and the others respond together. The chosen child must sit down while dancing. The game ends when all the children are seated. The one who did not hear their name called loses the game. The game can continue in reverse order, having each player stand in turn as their name is called. The song is accompanied by the gambusi, a plucked instrument in the lute family related to the Yemeni qanbüs. About a metre in length, it is sculpted from a single block of wood. The sound box is covered by a stretched piece of goatskin and the four strings are made of gut. Traditionally, it is used to accompany Sufi religious songs. Amina is the first name of the mother of Mohammed, some 98% of Comorians being Muslim.

Santa Amina	Saint Amina
Santa Amina yazidi	Saint Amina is the best
Yazidi elikoli	The best in the school
Kamna unipendra	You don't even come close
Kamna unipendra бo Nawali	You don't even come close, oh Nawal
Kantsi rihuone	Sit down so we can see you

24 Ny pangalana MADAGASCAR

Language Malagasy **Singer** Tiana Masselot

Running along the southeast coast of Madagascar, Canal des Pangalanes is a long succession of rivers of uneven depth. Boatmen use the canal to transport their goods (fish, produce, handcrafted objects, sugar cane, coffee, cloves and pepper) from one village to another, sometimes on single-hull craft like canoes made of a hollowed tree trunk propelled by paddle, sometimes by *lakana*, a traditional outrigger canoe with a triangular sail, as is the case here. Children participate in building these craft and learn to handle them from a young age. This song accompanies the rhythm of their paddles.

Madio manganohano mba tazano	See how the lovely bends in the Panagalan River
Ny fidoladolanan'ny Pangalana	Are clean and clear
Voizo manafo	Paddle, my friend
Andeha hanarato	Your canoe, my friend
Voizo manafo	To go fishing
Voizo	Paddle, my friend
	Paddle

25 La rivière Tanier MAURITIUS

Language Mauritian Creole Singers Jean Groeme and Hélène Groeme

All Mauritians know *La rivière Tanier*, a beautiful lullaby composed by Fery Kletzer, a Hungarian cellist born in 1830, during a visit to Réunion and Mauritius. It tells the story of a poor old woman reduced to fishing for tiny *cabos* just to survive. As in other cultures around the world, many lullabies echo life's difficulties. This one speaks of the Lataniers River, whose source is at the foot of Pieter Both Mountain. The river crosses several neighbourhoods in Port Louis, the Mauritian capital, before reaching the Indian Ocean. The expression "way, way" ("ow, ow") undoubtedly derives from "wayo," chanted by Senegalese slaves to express suffering and pain. To this day, there is a village named Camp Yoloff, a variant of "*wolof*," a West African ethnic group and language from Senegal. "*Way way, mes zenfants*" here means "Alas, alas, my children."

Mo passer la riviere Tanier	I went by Lataniers River
Mo zoine ene vié grand mama	Where I met an old grandma
Mo dire li ki li fer la	I asked her what she was doing there
Li dir moi li lapesse cabo	She said she was fishing chub
Way way, mes zenfants	Alas, alas, my children
Fo travay pou gagne son pain	One must work to earn one's living
Grand dimoune ki wa pé faire	"Old woman, what are you doing
Sa ki vié rest dans lacaz	Old people should stay home."
Li dir moi Moi bien mizere	She told me, "I am very poor
Mais mo ena tout mo couraz	But I have plenty of courage"
Way way, mes zenfants	Alas, alas, my children
Fo travay pou gagne son pain	One must work to earn one's living

Song selection, explanatory notes and vocal coordination Nathalie Soussana Illustrations Magali Attiogbé
Graphic Design Catherine Ea and Stephan Lorti for Haus Design Translation David Lytle and Hélène Roulston for
Service d'édition Guy Connolly Producer, arranger, recording, mixing and mastering Jean-Christophe Hoarau

Musicians Justin Vali (valiha), Yannick Legoff (flutes), Lionel Agenor (guitar), Tao Ravao (kabosy),
Adrien Espinouze (ney), Vincent Bellec (drums and percussions), Gilles Hoarau (percussions: kayamb, rouleur, sati,
piker, and bobre) and Jean-Christophe Hoarau (bass, gambusi, ndzendze, guitar, and percussions)

Singers Costa Neto, Nawal Mlanao, Tao Ravao, Nolitha Dlabhongo, Melissa Peter, Kamay Pelasimba, Lionel Agenor,
Éloïse Agenor-Poinsot, Ahlam Boina, Jean Groeme, Hélène Groeme, Tiana Masselot and Micheline Tamachia

Back-up singers Hadidja Alfeine, Nayah Cheny, Jean-Christophe Hoarau, Sophie Humblot, Mathilde Poinsot,
Mlinda Selemani, Nathalie Soussana, Ayane Teouri and Ichane Teouri

This work was published with the support of the Institut français's publishing program.

A unique code for the digital download of all recordings and a printable file of the illustrated lyrics is included with
this book-CD. All recordings, under the title *Comptines et berceuses de vanille*, are also available on several musical
streaming platforms.

℗ www.thesecretmountain.com
℗© 2021 The Secret Mountain (Folle Avoine Productions)
ISBN-13: 978-2-925108-70-2